For Jack

Library of Congress Cataloging in Publication Data

Taylor, Judy, 1932 –
Sophie and Jack.

Summary: Two hippopotamus friends go on a picnic and
play hide-and-seek, but have trouble finding a place to
hide, at first.
[1. Hippopotamus – Fiction. 2. Picnicking – Fiction.
3. Hide-and-seek – Fiction] I. Gantner, Susan, ill.
II. Title.
PZ7.T21476So 1982   [E]   82-13279
ISBN 0-399-20947-6

Sophie and Jack

JUDY TAYLOR

Illustrated by
Susan Gantner

PHILOMEL

New York

It was a wonderful day for a picnic.

Everyone was hungry.

Soon there was not much left.

"Let's play hide-and-seek," said Sophie.

"I'll hide," said Jack.

"I'll seek," said Sophie.

Jack hid behind a tree with his eyes shut tight.

Sophie shut her eyes, too, and counted to ten.

Sophie found Jack very quickly. "Now me," she said.

Jack turned his back and counted to ten.

Sophie hid in the grass with her eyes shut tight.

Jack found her very quickly.

"Me again," said Jack, and he ran off to hide.

Sophie couldn't find Jack anywhere.

Can you?